Start-Off StorieS

THE FROG PRINCE

By Mary Lewis Wang

Illustrated by Gwen Connelly

Prepared under the direction of Robert Hillerich, Ph.D.

CHILDRENS PRESS ®

CHICAGO

"My ball! My ball! I want
my ball!" said the Princess.

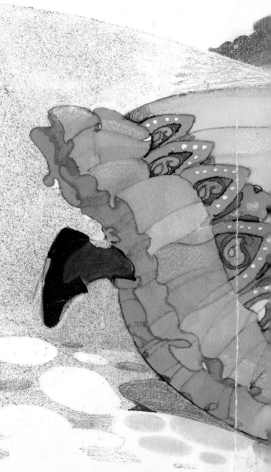

Library of Congress Cataloging-in-Publication Data

Wang, Mary Lewis.
 The frog prince.

 (Start-off stories)
 Summary: A retelling of the Grimm fairy tale in which a
frog retrieves the princess' ball for a promise that the princess
is reluctant to keep.
 [1. Fairy tales 2. Folklore—Germany] I. Title.
II. Series.
PZ8.W196Fr 1986   398.2'1'0943 [E]   86-11796
ISBN 0-516-03983-0

3

"Let me help you,
Princess," said a frog.
The Princess said,
"A frog cannot help."

The frog said, "I will
get your ball. But will you
do something for me?"
"I will! I will!" said
the Princess.

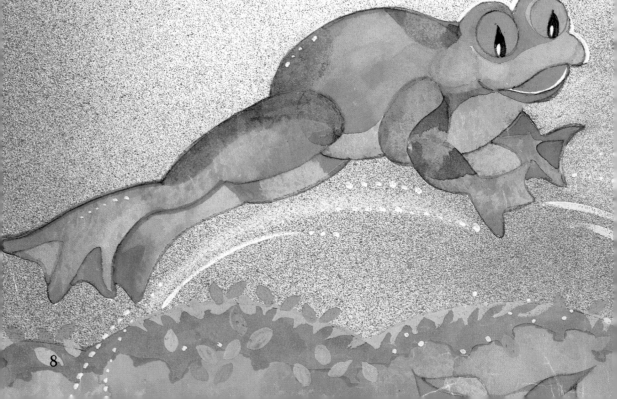

"Let me play with you in
your house," the frog said.
"Let me eat with you. Let
me sleep by you."

"Yes, yes! I promise!"
said the Princess.

So down went the frog.
Up came the ball.
The Princess took the
ball and ran.

"Stop!" said the frog.
"What about your promise?"
The frog ran after her.

11

"Let me in!" he said.

"No, Frog," said the Princess.

"But you promised!" said the frog.

"So I did," said the
Princess.
So the frog came in
to play.

The frog said, "That was fun. Now let me eat with you."

"No, Frog," said the Princess.

"But you promised!" said the frog.

"So I did," said the Princess.
So the frog came to eat.

"That was good," said the frog. "Now for a good sleep."

"No, Frog," said the Princess.

"But you promised!" said the frog.

"So I did," said the Princess. "Sleep there, but then get out of my house!"

ZAP! The frog was not
a frog.
He was a Prince!
"Oh!" said the Princess.
"Who are you?"

"I was a Prince," he said.

"But a wicked witch made me a frog.

"I was a frog for a long time.

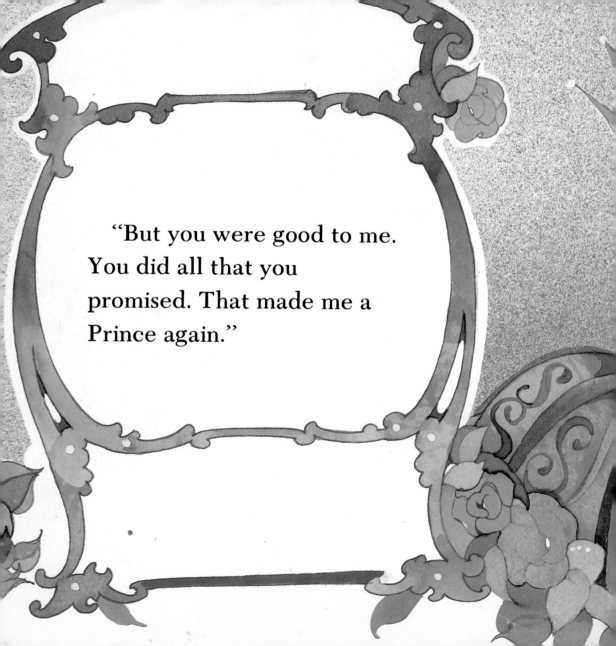

"But you were good to me. You did all that you promised. That made me a Prince again."

Everyone was happy.

WORD LIST

a	fun	oh	to
about	get	out	took
after	good	play	up
again	happy	Prince	want
all	he	Princess	was
and	help	promise	went
ball	her	promised	were
but	house	ran	what
by	I	said	who
came	in	sleep	wicked
cannot	let	so	will
did	long	something	witch
do	made	stop	with
down	me	that	yes
eat	my	the	you
everyone	no	then	your
for	now	there	zap
frog	of	time	

The vocabulary of *The Frog Prince* correlates with the following word lists: Dolch 81%, Hillerich 78%, Durr 84%.

ABOUT THE AUTHOR

Mary Lewis Wang has edited many books for children. Formerly an editor with McGraw-Hill Book Company, Golden Press, and John Wiley & Sons, she has also been a reporter-researcher for *Newsweek* magazine and a book reviewer for the *St. Louis Post-Dispatch.* A native New Yorker, she is now a resident of St. Louis, Missouri. She and her husband have raised three avid readers—probably the best preparation of all, she feels, for writing for children.

ABOUT THE ARTIST

Gwen Connelly was born in Chicago in 1952. After studying fine art at the University of Montana, she worked in various areas of commercial art. Since concentrating on children's publishing she has illustrated several story books, as well as contributed to numerous educational programs. Ms. Connelly lives in Highland Park, Illinois, with her husband, two children and four cats.